DREAMWORKS

Spirit

RIDING FREE

The Spring Filly!

DreamWorks Spirit Riding Free © 2020 DreamWorks Animation LLC.
All Rights Reserved.
Illustrations by Maine Diaz

Cover design by Ching Chan. Cover illustration by Maine Diaz.

Little, Brown and Company
Hachette Book Group
1290 Avenue of the Americas, New York, NY 10104
Visit us at LBYR.com

First Edition: February 2020

Little, Brown and Company is a division of Hachette Book Group, Inc. The Little, Brown name and logo are trademarks of Hachette Book Group, Inc.

The publisher is not responsible for websites (or their content) that are not owned by the publisher.

Library of Congress Control Number 2019947037

ISBNs: 978-0-316-45515-2 (pbk.), 978-0-316-45516-9 (ebook)

Printed in the United States of America

LSC-C

10 9 8 7 6 5 4 3 2

OFFICIAL
MARK OF
SPIRIT

DREAMWORKS
Spirit
RIDING FREE

The Spring Filly!

G. M. Berrow
Illustrated by Maine Diaz

Little, Brown and Company
New York Boston

Chapter 1

Lucky Prescott snuggled in under her soft comforter. A fresh spring breeze blew in through the open bedroom window and rustled her new blue gingham curtains. The sun wasn't even up yet, but it was already starting to get warm outside. Everyone was predicting that the next few months in Miradero were going to be warmer than usual, but Lucky didn't mind. The weather made it feel as if it were already summer, even though it was still a few weeks away. Lucky couldn't wait for the seasons to change. She was looking forward to spending the upcoming summer with her best friends, Pru and Abigail, riding their horses through their wondrous, well-trod trails before heading off to boarding school at Palomino Bluffs Riding Academy in the fall. They had it all planned out. The goal was to have as much fun as possible and go on even more horseback rides than last year. Plus, Lucky reasoned, what better way to beat the heat than feeling the wind in her hair when she broke into a gallop? Lucky was glad that her horse, Spirit, felt the same way.

After a quick yawn and stretch, Lucky quickly fell back into her sweet dreams of summer. She had barely begun snoring again when the clatter of something bouncing off her windowsill caused Lucky to bolt upright in bed. A small brown circle lay on her flowered rug, illuminated by the dim light of the early morning.

"What in the world could that be?" Lucky whispered to herself. She hopped out of bed and crouched down to inspect it. She picked up the circle and its crumbly edges began to break off in her hand. It was a biscuit! Not just *any* biscuit, either. It was one of Abigail's homemade horse treats. Before Lucky could investigate any further, another treat came barreling through the window and hit Lucky right in the shoulder! The treat exploded into a hundred oaty bits and made quite the crumbly mess. But Lucky couldn't help giggling as she shot over to the window and stuck out her head. "Abigail? Pru?" she whispered to her friends down below. "What are you guys doing here? It's practically the middle of the night!"

"Lucky, did you completely forget our plan?" Pru whispered back. Lucky racked her brain. Admittedly, her mind still felt a bit foggy with sleep.

"Plan?" Lucky replied. "Were we going to have a slumber party?"

"No! We're going on a dawn trail ride. I've been promising Boomerang that we'd watch the sunrise from his favorite spot for weeks!" Abigail answered, a little too loudly for the hour. "*And we brought breakfast.*" She patted the top of her wicker picnic basket. Lucky licked her lips, imagining what baked goodies Abigail had created this time. She knew it was still dark outside,  but Lucky couldn't help it. Whenever she woke up, she was immediately in search of a snack. It also didn't hurt that Abigail's knack for baking and sweets was unparalleled in Miradero.

"Oh yeah! Of course," Lucky replied with a grin. "Just give me two seconds and I'll see you downstairs!" Abigail and Pru gave a little cheer and clapped their hands in delight. *"Shhh!"* Lucky called out. She had already asked her dad and stepmother, Kate, for permission a few days ago, but she didn't want to wake them or her new baby sister, Polly. Once that baby woke up, she was all sorts of adorable trouble.

"Okay, it's been two seconds!" whisper-shouted Abigail in between fits of giggles. "Hurry up, Lucky!"

Lucky quickly dressed in her favorite outfit: saddle-worn jeans and a white top. But she waited to put on her shoes. She was careful to carry her cowgirl boots down the stairs, lest they clunk too loudly on the wooden steps. She grabbed her satchel and swept silently through the kitchen, tossing three crisp Rojo Delicioso apples, a block of cheddar cheese, and a canteen of water inside. Then she was out the door.

By the time Lucky, Abigail, and Pru arrived at the stables, Boomerang and Chica Linda were already making happy snorting sounds and pawing at their stall doors. Even Spirit had arrived and was pacing back and forth. Clearly, the horses were just as excited as the PALs and were gearing up to stretch their legs to ride free on the open trail.

"Don't worry, Boomerang," Abigail assured her pinto gelding with a loving pat. "We'll be out there in no time! Well, maybe a little time because you're not wearing your saddle yet. But it won't be *much* time. Anyway, I'm probably wasting time right

now talking about time this whole time...."
Abigail giggled and then nodded to Pru.
"Let's saddle up!" The two girls sprang
into action, giving their respective horses
a short brushdown and securing soft
blankets at the top of the horses' withers.
Then they took the brown leather saddles
off their racks and began to wrap the straps
around the horses' midsections. Spirit was
actually a wild and free horse, so Lucky
never used a saddle to ride him.

As Pru tightened the buckles on Chica
Linda's saddle, Lucky ran her fingers
through Spirit's silky mane. Even when he
got little tangles in it, Lucky was always
impressed by how soft it was. "There you
go, Spirit. Ready to ride?"

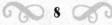

All three horses whinnied and kicked in response. Luckily, the barn was far enough from the Granger house that they didn't wake anyone. Lucky, Abigail, and Pru hopped on their horses and took off for the trails. Shivers of excitement ran down Lucky's spine as the fresh spring air hit her face. What a thrill!

By the time the girls reached the crested ridge of Hideaway Hill—one of the PALs' favorite secret spots—the sky was changing into a canvas of brilliant orange and three shades of pink.

"Over here!" Pru exclaimed as she lay out a blue-checked blanket. There was just enough time to set up the picnic breakfast before the sun began to peek over the

horizon. Lucky was just about to bite into
a warm biscuit slathered in butter when
she felt a familiar muzzle and warm breath
snorting in her ear. Spirit had bent down,
sniffing her to signal that he was hungry,
too.

"Whoops. How could I forget?" Lucky
laughed. She reached inside her satchel

and tossed the apples to Boomerang, Chica Linda, and Spirit. Three crunches later and the apples were completely gone. "Look, Spirit!" Lucky pointed at the painted sky. "Isn't Miradero beautiful? I hope we get sunrises like this at Palomino Bluffs."

"I'm sure we will, but we'll probably be way too tired from all our new classes to wake up and see them," Pru replied. "But let's not get too ahead of ourselves. Have you seen all the new badges the Frontier Fillies have to offer?" Pru pulled a booklet from her bag and began to flip through it. "There are so many new activities to try! They even have dressage! Do you think I can earn the advanced badge?" Even though Pru was new to the sport, she'd had

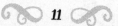

lots of experience training horses in the rodeo style.

"Absolutely!" Abigail chirped through a bite of cheese. "Your dressage skills have gotten better and better, Pru. Soon, you'll be a rodeo *and* dressage champion. You'll be so famous that people will want your autograph and Chica Linda's hoof-stamp."

"We're going to need a pretty big ink pad for that." Lucky nodded in agreement. "But I'm sure we can find one." If it hadn't been for some sneaky behavior on the part of one of the other competitors, Pru might have won her recent dressage competition. But that was all in the past. Now the PALs were looking ahead—and their future in the Frontier Fillies and at Palomino Bluffs

Riding Academy looked as bright as the sunrise!

"What else can we try? *Oooh*, look Boomerang! Intermediate mane-braiding!" Abigail called out. Boomerang responded with an exasperated snort. The three girls leafed through the pages of the booklet together, circling the activities they were interested in.

Suddenly, Lucky's eyes landed on a gold emblem that looked like a sheriff's badge. On it were the words *Trail Trainer*. Lucky pointed excitedly. "Trail Trainers!"

"What's that?" Abigail scrunched her nose inquisitively.

"I actually don't know," Lucky admitted. "But whatever it is, I think we need to do it.

It looks official and important. Just look at that shiny symbol."

Pru cleared her throat and read aloud: "'To become a Frontier Fillies certified Trail Trainer, the Filly must display the utmost poise and proficiency for horse training. Candidates will complete and present a demonstration to prove that they have mastered the necessary skills for training an unfamiliar horse. Some example tasks include: cleaning hooves, bathing, haltering, leading, and groundwork as well as various more advanced voice commands associated with riding horses, packhorses, performing horses, and draft horses.'"

"An unfamiliar horse?" Abigail asked. "Like Boomerang in a silly costume? He definitely has experience as a performing horse from when he was in the *El Circo Dos Grillos* with Pru."

"I think that it means you *can't* use Boomerang." Pru shrugged. "That way they know you can train *any* horse instead of just the one you already have." She pointed at the booklet. "Whoa. It also says here that Trail Trainers get all sorts of cool privileges like first pick of campsites at Jamborees."

"What? That's incredible! We have to do it," Abigail insisted. "From PALs to Trail Trainers!" She held up her water canteen in a "cheers" motion. But nobody joined in.

"Wait a second...you have to be able to train *any* horse?" Lucky's excitement began to drain out of her. She regarded Spirit.

Watching him stand there with his strong muscles and his kind face gave Lucky a sense of pride. But he was a wild horse. Lucky had certainly learned to ride him, but not in the usual way. It was as if they had their own language, and it was anything but traditional. She couldn't really call it "training." In fact, Lucky had never really learned to properly train a horse at all.

"What's wrong, Lucky?" Pru asked, reading the conflicted expression in Lucky's eyes.

"It's just that...maybe you and Abigail should try to become Trail Trainers without me. You two have experience in traditional training. Spirit and I have...our own way of doing things." Lucky slumped down.

"That's probably not what they're looking for."

"Lucky, are you even hearing yourself?" Pru replied. "Spirit is a wild horse and you ride him without a saddle! That's amazing! I think you can definitely handle learning some basics. Plus, Abigail and I will teach you."

"Really?" Lucky brightened. "Even if we have to start with the super-easy stuff?"

Abigail nodded and smiled. "I think we all could use a refresher. We can start first thing tomorrow! Maybe not *this* early, though..." Boomerang and Chica Linda stomped the ground in agreement. Spirit nuzzled Lucky as if to say he liked the idea, too.

Pru, Abigail, and Lucky all cheered. It was settled. They were going to ace the Trail Trainers test, and they were going to do it as they did everything—together. Now all they had to do was find some willing horses to teach. "Come on!" urged Lucky. "Let's go find Kate! Maybe she'll let us borrow Tambourine."

Chapter 2

The girls galloped all the way back to Miradero, partially because they were trying to beat the heat, but also because they were so excited by their new goal. By the time they'd reached the ramada, Al Granger was packing up his saddlebags and getting his horse's tack ready. He looked surprised to see them. "What are you three doing up already?"

"Remember, Dad?" Pru rolled her eyes. "Sunrise trail ride?" She was pretty sure he was just pretending to have forgotten, since it had been the only thing she'd talked about all week.

"Oh right." Al smiled to himself. "Were the sights as breathtaking as you girls hoped?"

"Even better," replied Abigail. She swung her leg over Boomerang's back and hopped down from the stirrup. "The sky looked just like Lucky's shirt after that time Polly threw her mashed sweet potatoes at her! Orange splotches everywhere..."

"Sounds, uh...stunning." Al chuckled. He hoisted up a bag and secured it to the side of his horse's saddle. "Well, I'm glad you had fun. I'd love to stay and chat longer, but I'd better get a move on. I've got to get there early if I want to bid on a good horse."

"Get where early, Mr. Granger?" Lucky asked, ears perked up. Did he just say he was going to get a new horse? *New horses need to be trained!* thought Lucky. *Training a new horse would be* way *better than borrowing Kate's horse.*

"I'm heading over to the Silverlode Spring Equine Auction," Al replied. "It's

much bigger than the one in Cannon City. I'm going to find a new draft horse for the ramada. It'll be good to have a big, strong horse around to lend a helping hoof."

Immediately, all three girls looked at one another. They didn't even need to say anything to know what the others were thinking: Nevermind Tambourine—they'd find a horse of their own! "Dad! Let us tag along!" Pru begged, putting on her sweetest face. "Please?"

Al hesitated. "I don't know, girls....It's a long trip and I need to stay focused on my goal."

"We won't be any trouble. In fact, we can help you find the best horse to bid on!" Pru insisted. She could be very convincing

when she wanted to be and, as a result, Al Granger found it *very* hard to resist his daughter's charms. He looked to Lucky and Abigail, raising his eyebrows, then back at Pru. He sighed and shook his head with a chuckle, defeated. "All right, you girls can come. But remember—eyes on the prize. We have a job to do."

"We won't let you down," Lucky said with a smile.

The Silverlode Spring Equine Auction was bustling with activity. The last time the girls had been somewhere so crowded was when they'd visited Calliope Bay to meet Madame Gummery, the headmistress of

Tides Run. Lucky was supposed to have had an interview for the academy, but kept managing to embarrass herself in front of the headmistress. It had all turned out okay in the end, but Lucky just hoped that their adventure today would go smoother than that one.

"Look at all of these beauties!" Pru exclaimed to her friends as they followed

behind Al, trotting along on Chica Linda, Boomerang, and Spirit. "We're definitely going to find you a good horse here, Dad." Sure enough, tons of gorgeous horses of varying breeds and sizes were everywhere they looked. Most of the animals were either being groomed by their sellers or led to the auction stalls. The air was sweet with the scent of warm hay and sunshine.

Lucky, Abigail, and Pru were careful to give their own horses reassuring pats to remind them that they were only here on a mission to buy a horse, not sell one. Spirit, especially, got nervous in situations like this since he'd been wrangled himself, first by Mr. Granger's mesteñeros, then again by Harlan Grayson. The mischievous man had even sold Spirit in the Cannon City auction, so it was understandable that he might feel a bit tense.

"It's okay, boy," Lucky assured him. "I won't let anyone auction you ever again." Spirit responded with a satisfied snort. "Now, let's go rack up over there!" Lucky pointed to an empty horse rack standing apart from the auction stalls.

"All right, I'm gonna go survey the options," Al said, hopping off his horse and racking up next to Chica Linda, Boomerang, and Spirit. He gave the PALs a wink. "You three stay out of trouble, now. Remember our deal, okay?"

Lucky, Abigail, and Pru nodded in unison and waved to Al as he disappeared into the bobbing sea of cowboy hats and horses. Then they took off for the covered stalls, eager to inspect all the beautiful horses for sale. Abigail also had her sights set on the popcorn stall, so they had to stop there first.

"Look at this guy," Lucky said, drawn immediately to a sturdy stallion with a mottled brown-and-white hide. He tossed back his shiny mane and let out a friendly greeting as the girls approached him.

"He looks strong," Abigail remarked through a mouthful of buttered kernels. "And a little like Boomerang. I like him."

"Let's see a little more about you, buddy," Pru said to the horse, inspecting the handwritten stat card, which hung from a little rope on the front of his stall gate. "Just as I thought! He's an Appaloosa. Appaloosas *are* known for their tractability, good sense, and remarkable stamina. Might be a good option." Pru was taking her mission very seriously.

In the next stall, a reddish-brown mare with a cropped mane was munching on some hay and eyeing the PALs. Abigail

skipped over just to see if she was as soft as she looked. "*Aww,* I like her. She's perfect for Mr. Granger! Don't you think?"

"I'm not sure." Pru joined her and began to pet the gentle mare's muzzle. "She's a Morgan—they definitely have a sweet disposition and are pretty hardy. But I think my dad is looking for something even bigger...." While Pru and Abigail debated the merits of the Morgan horse, something in the far right of the stables caught Lucky's eye.

The stallion must have been about eighteen hands high—a full three hands higher than Spirit. He was a rich brown color, with a white blaze down the front of his muzzle. When he stomped his hooves, his furry white fetlocks swung around like giant tassels. He was magnificent. Even the shafts of sunlight seemed to stream in and illuminate his stall as if a spotlight were shining on him.

Lucky gasped in awe. "Pru! Abigail! There he is! That's the horse we're looking for!"

The three girls bounded over to meet the towering Clydesdale. "His name is Buster!" Lucky exclaimed, reading his stat card.

Abigail craned her neck to look up at the huge horse from below his chin. He sniffed at her and then licked a wayward piece of popcorn off her shirt. "Whoa."

"We did it! We found the perfect horse."

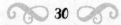

Pru clapped her hands together in delight. "I'm going to find my dad. Buster is definitely the one."

But before Pru could leave, there was a loud *CRASH*! Bits of dust kicked up around Buster as the noise repeated, growing even louder. Buster seemed to be standing still, but was somehow rattling the wood panels of his own stall. It was almost as if he were going to bust right out and run away. *Maybe that's how he got his name!* Lucky thought.

"Look! It's not Buster doing that." Pru pointed to the space behind Buster's hind legs. "It's a tiny horse!" Suddenly, a little cream-colored muzzle appeared and quickly disappeared again. Buster whinnied. Then he spun around to reveal a small, stout, flaxen-colored horse with a blond mane jumping and kicking around in the back of the stall. The little horse kicked her hooves playfully, flinging hay into the air. Buster let out a heavy sigh. He seemed used to this routine and had little patience with it.

"Is that a pony?!" Abigail shrieked. Her smile reached from ear to ear.

"No, I'm afraid not, ma'am," said an unfamiliar voice, causing all three girls to jump in surprise. "Not a pony. But she *is* a li'l devil. And if I were you, I'd stay far, far away."

Chapter 3

"Sorry, didn't mean to startle ya!" The speaker chuckled and tilted back his white cowboy hat. "I've been told I have a flair for the dramatic." He smiled underneath his bushy red beard and mustache. He shook his head apologetically as he approached the stall. "I'm Mr. Rollins, that's Buster, and that little gal there is Sandy."

"Awww..." Abigail leaned over the edge of the stall. "Hi, Sandy!"

"Don't let looks deceive ya. She's the

wildest mini horse I've ever owned. Had to bring her to the auction today just to keep an eye on her while I'm away from my barn! Otherwise, I'd probably come home to a pile of planks and rubble. Isn't that right, Buster?"

Buster gave a little nod, but he could have just been looking for a snack instead of agreeing.

"Really?" Lucky replied, regarding the cream-colored horse. "But she's so...itty-bitty."

"You'd be surprised. She's incredibly strong and packs a big punch when she wants to. Doesn't want to be trained, either. Do you, girl?" Mr. Rollins opened the gate and whistled. At this, Sandy whinnied, then did a little spin. She was clearly trying her best to look cute. "That's about as far as we've gotten, and it's not good for much." Mr. Rollins laughed and wiped the sweat from his brow. "But enough about Sandy. Were you interested in Buster?"

Once the girls located Al Granger, he immediately fell in love with the Clydesdale. While he busied himself with getting acquainted with Mr. Rollins and asking all the necessary questions, Lucky saw her opportunity. She wondered if Pru and Abigail had the same idea that she did. There was no doubt about the fact that Buster was the perfect specimen—strong and big. Just what they were looking for. But Lucky couldn't get Sandy out of her head. She was clearly a handful, but maybe she didn't have to be. Not with their help!

Lucky quickly pulled Pru and Abigail aside to an empty stall for an impromptu PALs meeting. She spoke in hushed tones. Luckily, all the hay around them helped deaden the sound. "We need a new horse to train to become Trail Trainers, right? And Sandy needs training—desperately! Let's ask Mr. Rollins if we can bid on Sandy. It's perfect. What do you guys think?"

A moment passed before anyone said anything. Lucky held her breath as she waited. Finally, Pru raised an eyebrow and admitted, "Well, the timing *is* perfect...."

"And she's just so *cute*!" Abigail added. "How hard could it be?"

"Not as hard as it will be convincing my dad to let us bid on Sandy," Pru retorted. She paused for a second, considering. "But that's never stopped me before. Let's do it!"

"Trail Trainers, here we come!" Lucky cheered. "Okay, we have to hurry." They didn't have much time. Buster was set to go to the auction stage soon. The girls knew that as soon as Al bid and won his horse, they'd have to leave Silverlode.

Sure enough, when they rushed back over to the corner stall, Mr. Rollins was trying to untie Buster's rope. Sandy put her head right in the way of where Mr. Rollins was trying to reach each time he extended his arm. The little horse had her mouth open and kept nibbling at the rope, causing

quite the added difficulty for all three of
them. Buster flicked his tail and turned his
ears back in annoyance.

"What a troublemaker!" Al Granger
laughed. "Good luck getting that filly off
your hands today."

"Oh, I'm not even going to put her up
for auction," Mr. Rollins admitted. Finally,
the cowboy was able to untie the rope and

get a harness on the
horse. He began to
lead Buster out of the
stall, but Sandy ran
between the stallion's
legs and blocked
him. "No one would
bid on her, anyhow."

"Except us!" Pru blurted out. "We want to bid on Sandy."

"Oh boy." Al crossed his arms over his chest and met his daughter's eyes. "Didn't we have a deal today?"

"Deal?" Pru echoed innocently. "Oh, yeah, 'stay focused on the goal.' But, um... see, well, we have a side goal now, too."

Al raised his eyebrows. "*Side* goal?"

Pru motioned to her friends and her words all came spilling out at once. "The three of us want to become Frontier Fillies Trail Trainers, but to do that, we need to teach Lucky how to train a horse from scratch and Sandy is the perfect horse for the job! Between the three of us, we have a little money saved up from our apple baked goods sales and horse washes, so we can put in a bid ourselves."

"Whoa there, little filly!" Mr. Rollins put up his hands in a "stop" motion. "Let's just back it up for a second."

Lucky was sure that Mr. Rollins was about to tell them their idea was out of the question, but instead he tilted his head to the side and asked, "Where did you all say you're from again?"

"Miradero," Mr. Granger replied. "Do you know it?"

"Sure do." Mr. Rollins nodded. "In fact, I'll be heading out that way in a couple of weeks for the Founders' Day Parade. I've got some...business to attend to for the parade," he said vaguely. Of course,

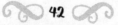

Lucky and her friends knew all about the upcoming parade that featured famous "front-row" horseback riders who were chosen each year to play the parts of the Miradero founders. Abigail and Pru had always wanted to be picked, but the honor usually went to much more skilled riders.

"Tell you what"—Mr. Rollins pulled a piece of hay from his vest pocket and began to chew on it. He narrowed his eyes, wheels clearly turning in his mind—"if you girls can train Sandy by then, you can keep her. But if she's not up to snuff, I'll have to take her back for her own good. Who knows—maybe you'll have better luck than me."

"We can take her home with us? Just

like that?" Lucky asked, trying to contain her excitement.

"Well, you seem like responsible young horse wranglers." Mr. Rollins turned to Al. "What do you think, Dad? Are they trustworthy?"

"They *are* a little too impulsive...." The stern look on Al Granger's face melted away. "But yes, they're trustworthy." He sighed with a chuckle. "It's not too much trouble for you?"

"Actually, you'd be doing me a favor. I love the little gal, but I have a lot of horses to keep me busy. She clearly needs some extra attention."

"Now, *that* we can do!" said Pru as she, Abigail, and Lucky rushed over to pet

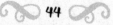

Sandy. She tried to lick their hands, looking for wayward popcorn. "How much do we owe you?"

"Did I hear you say you're bakers?" asked Mr. Rollins with a little wink.

"Yes, sir!" Abigail chirped. "Apple pies, apple turnovers, Apple Abigails, horse oat biscuits, scones, biscuits for people, cookies, brownies—"

"In that case," Mr. Rollins interrupted, "how does one apple pie sound?"

A new mini horse to train for the price of one little baked dessert? Lucky could hardly believe her good fortune. "Sounds like you've got yourself a pretty sweet deal, Mr. Rollins!"

Chapter 4

After the journey home from Silverlode, the PALs were exhausted. With the two extra horses in tow, it had taken almost twice as long for the gang to herd themselves back to Miradero. Al's new stallion, Buster, was steady and strong, just as predicted. The Clydesdale was totally unfazed by the long walk and easily kept pace with Spirit, Boomerang, and Chica Linda.

But Sandy was another story.

The mini horse pulled and tugged at her

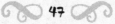

ropes and constantly tried to gallop in the opposite direction. Sometimes she would just sit down in the middle of the trail and start chewing on weeds. Mr. Granger was skeptical of Sandy's potential. "I hope you girls know what you got yourselves into," he said. "The Founders' Day Parade will come up sooner than you think."

It was going to be a lot of work to train her. But Lucky felt excited about trying.

They'd even set up a special corner of the barn just for her—Sandy-proofed. Lucky had brought a bunch of old pillows from her house and secured them to the walls so that the rowdy horse could twirl and kick without breaking anything. Buster was content in his stall up front, far away

from his pesky "little sister." Sandy and all the other horses were also resting for the moment. Even Spirit was perched in his stall with his eyes closed.

"It's a pity we couldn't have just let Sandy take a piggyback ride on Buster's back," joked Abigail as she brushed Boomerang. "He's big enough to carry anything!"

"I don't think training horses to ride

other horses was what Mr. Rollins meant by 'training Sandy,'" Pru reasoned. She filled Chica Linda's water trough and used the pitchfork from the corner to replenish her stall with fresh hay. "But now that I think about it...what *did* he mean?"

"I'm too tired to even think about it right now," Abigail replied as she collapsed onto a hay bale.

"Me too," admitted Lucky. "And I've got to get home before dinner. I promised my dad and Kate that I'd set the table." Lucky regretted having to tear herself away from her new project, but it was probably important for everyone to get some rest. Until then, Lucky would just have to be patient. It was not her strongest suit.

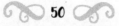

The next morning, Lucky was the first one to the barn. If she'd been allowed to spend the night there, she probably would have. So when Lucky swung open the door, she couldn't help feeling as if it were Christmas morning and she was about to open her presents. But she had to contain her enthusiasm. She didn't want to wake the other horses, who were snoozing peacefully.

"Sandy?" Lucky whispered as she crept past the stalls. "Where are you, little girl?" But the mini horse was not in her corner. All that was there was a big pile of hay. That was peculiar. Maybe she'd broken into Buster's stall. She *was* used to sharing with the Clydesdale after all. But a quick survey determined that Buster was still fast asleep and enjoying his own personal space.

Panic was starting to rise in Lucky, but she stayed calm. "Sandy?" she whispered again. "I brought an apple for you!" Suddenly, the pile of hay in the corner began to rustle! A muzzle popped out of the top, nostrils sniffing. The hay fell away as Sandy stood up and trotted over to Lucky.

"What a strange creature you are!" Lucky laughed as she petted Sandy's mane. Sandy pushed her muzzle under Lucky's armpit. "Oh right, your apple. Here!" It took the mini horse three bites to eat the treat, as opposed to Spirit, who could chomp one whole. "At least we know you're food-motivated. That'll help us in training. Are you ready for your big day?"

Sandy's quizzical look implied that she had no idea of what was about to happen. That made two of them. "Don't worry," Lucky said, more for herself than the horse. "We'll figure it out."

A few hours later, Pru and Abigail finally joined Lucky in the barn. The rest of the horses were awake by then, munching on hay and stomping around in their stalls. Lucky was raring to go, too. She had spent the whole morning reading a book called *How to Train Your Packhorse: A Practical Guide*. She'd come across it in a stack of Kate's books back home. Maybe it would be of some help to them today.

"Lucky Prescott—are you *studying*?" Pru teased. Lucky tossed the book to Pru. Abigail appeared behind her shoulder. They quickly leafed through the pages. "I'm not sure if Sandy is really a packhorse, but it's a start."

"But that's the thing, isn't it?" Lucky

pointed out. "We don't really know *what* kind of horse she is yet. All we know is that she's small, strong, adorable, and spunky!"

"She makes a good point," admitted Abigail. "Especially the spunky part."

They led Sandy out to the ramada—the enclosure where they trained with their horses—and looked to Lucky. "So, what should we try first?" Pru asked. "I would know where to start if we were training her to do basic runs with a rider, but I'm not sure about packing."

Abigail considered this and came up short as well. "What does the book say, Lucky?"

But before Lucky could open her mouth and answer, Sandy took off at a wild gallop around the enclosure! She wriggled and bucked her legs out behind her like a rodeo horse. Her whinnies were accompanied by kicks and clouds of dust that covered the PALs. Sandy was acting like a wild horse, and, oddly enough, seemed to be enjoying how stunned the girls looked.

"Whoa, girl!" Lucky called as she chased after the little runaway. She caught up to Sandy and procured a sugar cube from her pocket. The filly came to a screeching halt. Lucky had Sandy's attention; now she just had to keep it. "Good, Sandy. Good horse... that's it..." she cooed, leading her back over to Pru and Abigail. Sandy lapped up the sugar and twirled around in a circle happily.

"She likes sugar *almost* as much as I do," Abigail joked. "Do you have any more of those, Lucky? I could use a treat."

Lucky sighed with a smile. "If we put in a full day of training, maybe we'll go get ice cream. For now, we've gotta focus!"

Now that Sandy was settled, Lucky read aloud from her book. "'First you must saddle the horse with a packsaddle so that he can get used to the breeching around his rump. Then lunge the horse or run him in a pen.'"

The girls couldn't find a packsaddle—or any saddle, for that matter—that was small enough to fit Sandy's tiny frame. They decided to use a pile of woven blankets meant to act as saddle pads instead. Pru

folded the
blankets to a
smaller size
and then tied
the short stack
around Sandy's
middle with
two leather girth straps. As long as they
kept feeding Sandy sugar cubes, she stayed
relatively still while they got her ready.

After a few runs around the ramada,
Sandy seemed to be catching on a little.
Maybe she *was* destined to be a packhorse.
At any rate, Lucky was eager to keep going.
If their work kept running so smoothly,
they would have Sandy trained well before
the Miradero Founders' Day Parade! Who

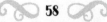

knew that becoming a Trail Trainer would be so easy?

"Next it says to fill some baskets with small rocks and tie them to either side of her packsaddle," Lucky explained. "Or I guess, her blanket stack." She remembered thinking that instruction was a bit strange.

"Why the rocks?" Abigail asked. "Won't the noise spook her?"

"That's sort of the point. It's to get her used to carrying things around, and used to the sound of whatever she is carrying," Pru said as she pointed to the open page. "Packhorses never know what sort of cargo they will have to carry."

The PALs fed Sandy some carrots while they looked around the ramada, choosing the smoothest rocks they could find. A couple of picnic baskets swiped from the kitchen acted as the cargo containers.

Once they attached them to either side of Sandy's body, she was calm for a moment. But, after hearing the rocks shift against one another, she took off across the pen as if her tail were on fire! The rocks clattered around in the baskets, sounding as if Sandy were playing two giant maracas! She kicked and writhed and twirled, until finally she galloped right at the fence and brushed against it, causing the baskets and blankets to fly off her body. Rocks went soaring through the air and landed like tiny meteorites in the dirt. Then Sandy sniffed the ground for sugar cubes as if none of it had just happened. Maybe this wouldn't be exactly as easy as Lucky had thought.

"Guess she's not a packhorse." Abigail sighed.

"Do you think she's a riding horse?" asked Lucky.

"We could try leading and groundwork," Pru suggested. "But we don't have tack small enough to fit her." Pru frowned. "Or a rider who is small enough to ride her."

"That's where you're wrong!" a squeaky little voice responded.

"Snips!" Abigail stomped over to the freckled little boy who had suddenly appeared on the fence. She groaned. "What are you doing here?"

"Came to see what all the commotion was." He leaned over the wooden railing and offered Sandy a carrot. The horse neighed, chomped down on the offering with one bite, then began to sniff Snips's hair for more hidden treats. "Señor Carrots and I were just minding our own business when we heard a whole bunch of it." Snips took a bite of a fresh carrot. "You oughta train that horse."

"We're trying." Lucky groaned. Then she furrowed her brow. "Wait—do you actually think you could ride her, Snips? It would really help us with her training."

"No, ma'am. No way I'm getting on that little horse." Snips shook his head. "But I know someone who probably would."

Pru and Abigail seemed unsure of Lucky's plan. They knew she was desperate to prove herself by becoming a Trail Trainer, but involving Snips in the process was a whole new barrel of apples. However, it didn't change the fact that they had promised Al Granger and Mr. Rollins that they would be responsible for Sandy's training. After all the begging she'd had to do, Pru couldn't just quit on the first day!

"Okay," Pru said with a determined nod. "But first we need something for the rider to ride *on*. Let's go visit Turo. We can use the money we saved up for custom Sandy-size tack. Then we can move on to more circle work and lunging. Then, who knows? After she gets used to the saddle, I might even be able to get Sandy to do some dressage moves!"

"Turo will know what to make!" Abigail echoed. Their friend was a very talented blacksmith and leathersmith. He'd even made Chica Linda's saddle when Pru was only eight years old. "Let's go! It's only two weeks, one day, and three hours until Sandy has to be trained for Mr. Rollins at the Founders' Day Parade!"

Chapter 5

The blacksmith was only about ten minutes
from Pru's stables, but the horses were
desperate to go for a walk. Pru measured
Sandy for her saddle while Lucky helped
Abigail tack up Boomerang and Chica Linda.
Spirit was spending some time with his herd,
so Lucky would go on foot. Everyone agreed
that it would be best if Sandy stayed behind
in the barn to get some rest after all that
rearing and bucking. Also, they didn't want
to chase her through the streets of Miradero.

When they arrived at the shop, they saw Turo was already busy helping another customer. Lucky noticed that the girl, who was about the PALs' age, was sitting in a wheelchair. She had shiny black hair plaited into twin braids and wore a pale-green dress that complemented her deep-brown eyes. She had a friendly face, but a shy demeanor. Lucky couldn't be sure, but she thought she'd seen her around Miradero before.

"I'll be with you ladies in just a moment," Turo said as he smiled and waved to Lucky, Abigail, and Pru. "Just finishing up with Caroline here." Turo made some notes in his ledger and handed her a ticket. "I should have that new set of horseshoes for your grandmother ready by next week. By the way, these are my friends Lucky, Abigail, and Pru."

"It's a pleasure to meet you." Caroline smiled. She thanked Turo and wheeled toward the door.

"Let me get that for you!" Abigail reached around her and pushed the door open.

"Thanks," Caroline said, ducking her head shyly. She looked as if she wanted to say more, but instead just added, "See you around." She wheeled herself out.

Lucky and the others quickly filled Turo in on their unusual needs. He would need to craft a custom miniature saddle, bridle, bit, and headstall. Since he was their friend (and loved a challenge), Turo gave them a discount and promised to get started right away. "Shouldn't take too long if these measurements you've given me are correct. Are you sure she's this little?"

"Yup, definitely. Checked them twice just to be sure," assured Pru. After spending her whole life around horses, she had learned some very unusual equestrian-related skills. Turo had a lot of work to do, so the girls said a quick good-bye.

Caroline was still outside. She was entranced by Boomerang and Chica Linda. She reached up to pet their silken manes and kept giggling every time they snorted near her head.

"Caroline, right? Lucky remarked. She pointed to the horses. "They're cute, huh?"

"Adorable!" Caroline nodded. "What are their names?"

"That's my horse, Boomerang, and Pru's horse, Chica Linda," said Abigail as she pointed to each. "Want to feed them some biscuits?" She procured a wax paper square from her pocket and unfolded it to reveal a neat stack of oat biscuits.

Caroline happily obliged. "I've always wanted a horse. You guys must have so much fun taking care of them! Especially during the summertime." Caroline sighed. There was sadness in her voice. "This whole summer is going to be so...boring."

"Why's that?" wondered Lucky.

"Well"—Caroline sighed again—"I just got to Miradero. I always spend the summer here with my grandparents. This year was going to be special. My cousin William and I were even going to build a Founders' Day Parade float to kick off the summer...but *he* got stuck with a bunch of makeup work so he doesn't end up in summer school, and now *I'm* stuck reading and teaching piano lessons."

Abigail handed Caroline a few more biscuits so Boomerang would stop trying to lick the poor girl's braids. "That doesn't sound so bad."

"It's all right, but I still really wish I was spending my time planning for the Founders' Day Parade. I just love the beautiful floats, and I've wanted to be in it ever since the first time I saw it," Caroline admitted wistfully.

"Tell me about it!" Pru agreed. "The parade is the best! I remember when I was seven, Mr. Winthrop made this float that looked like a giant ice cream sundae. The people who rode on it threw saltwater taffy out to us. Ugh, my mouth is watering just *thinking* about it! Someday, I hope Chica Linda and I will be chosen to ride in the front."

"Me too!" Abigail blurted out. "But teaching piano seems fun, too, though."

Caroline smiled, but her eyes kept darting back to the horses. "Oh, it is! It's really exciting when a student finally learns to play a melody! When the notes just click for them—there's nothing like it."

Lucky knew exactly what she meant. That's why she was so eager to teach Sandy. She was positive the horse would become well-trained with a little time and effort. Plus, that time and effort could turn Lucky

into a great
trainer as well.
"Practice makes
perfect, right?"

"Exactly.
Practice, practice,
practice!" said
Caroline, trying
to hold back her

giggles. But it wasn't because what Lucky
said was funny. It was because Boomerang
was licking the crumbs off her hands and it
tickled. She seemed to be a natural with the
horses. "Boomerang, you're so silly!"

"Hey, you should come by my dad's
stables sometime and meet the others,"
offered Pru.

"Definitely..." Lucky added, thinking of today's training with Sandy and how it had gone so differently than she'd hoped. "But maybe you'd better give us a few days first. Our new horse is, um...how do I put it lightly?" Lucky bit her lip. "A little unruly."

But that could all change with a little practice, practice, practice.

Chapter 6

"Special delivery!" Turo held up a shiny new saddle and accessories, beaming with pride. He sized up Sandy and broke out in a wide smile. "Wow, you weren't kidding. That horse really is tiny and cute."

It had been only three days since Lucky, Abigail, and Pru had placed their order, but it felt like three weeks. Every morning, they'd gotten up early to train Sandy and stopped only for lunch. They couldn't do much except lead her with a rope around the run and work on touch exercises, brushing her mane and hide to build trust. That is, when they could get her to hold still. She had so much energy for such a little horse that she was exhausting all three of them as well as the rest of the horses in the barn. The PALs didn't care to admit it, but the path to becoming a Trail Trainer required a lot more work than they'd bargained for.

"It really is a pity Sandy won't just keep the baskets on her back," Abigail had lamented on the second day, after their seventh attempt at the exercise. "She's so strong, she could definitely be a packhorse if she just put her mind to it!" They'd tried putting other items instead of rocks inside the baskets; everything from stuffed animals to books to oat cookies. That last idea had proven to be a really poor choice. Sandy had just immediately flung the baskets across the ramada and cantered around, eating the snacks off the ground while the girls stood there laughing.

But today would be different. It was time to try Sandy with a rider.

"Thank you, Turo!" Lucky squealed as she rushed to inspect the goods. It was well-known in Miradero that everything Turo made was of top-notch quality—and these were no exception. The rich brown leather of the miniature saddle was even stamped with the letters of Sandy's name on the back. The bridle and bit were just her size and made with extra care. "They're perfect."

"Well, let's try them on first before you say that," Turo said with a laugh. He stepped up onto the wooden rail of the fence and hoisted himself over it into the pen.

Sandy was busy munching on some weeds near a stack of barrels. Pru coaxed her over to Turo with a slice of apple. The little horse responded immediately. She trotted happily, shaking her mane and doing her signature spin on the way. But as Lucky and Abigail slid the bridle and headstall over Sandy's tawny muzzle, she began to writhe around as if the thing were made of snakes instead of soft, molded leather.

"Whoa, girl. It's all right now," Turo

assured her with a gentle pat. "That's it."

The saddle was a little easier to secure than the bridle, but Sandy still didn't like it. She started wriggling around and kicking her back legs out unhappily.

"*That's* the horse you expect one of us to ride?" a voice asked.

The PALs turned and saw Snips, Bianca, and Mary Pat walking toward the pen.

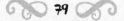

"Snips, what are they doing here?" Abigail asked.

"I said I knew someone who could ride your little horse. Here are *two* someones!" Snips replied.

"Yeah, except there's no way we're getting on that little thing," Mary Pat said. "Right, Bianca?" Bianca frowned and looked from the horse to Snips and back again. "*Right*, Bianca?!" Mary Pat urged.

"Well...she won't throw me, will she?" Bianca asked.

"She won't," Pru assured her.

"If Snips wants me to ride this little horse, then I'll do it!" Bianca declared. Mary Pat sighed heavily and rolled her eyes.

"All right, just nice and steady now,"

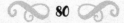

Lucky reminded the nervous girl. "Slow."

Bianca stepped forward and carefully mounted Sandy. She gently nudged the horse's sides with her feet and Sandy began to walk. Bianca managed to guide Sandy around the pen almost twice before everything fell apart. Sandy stopped to munch some more weeds and refused to listen to any commands. Nothing Bianca tried seemed to work.

"I know how to make this horse walk!" Snips hollered. He raised a stick above his head. A carrot tied to a long string was attached to the end of it. The idea was that the horse would try to reach the carrot with her mouth and would, in turn, walk forward. It worked on some horses and Snips's

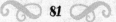

donkey, Señor Carrots. Bianca was hesitant, but she took the stick from Snips. As she dangled the carrot in front of the horse, Sandy took off in a canter, trying in vain to reach the treat. When the horse couldn't get it, she ran even faster and broke out

into a full gallop. But there was nowhere in the pen for her to go. Sandy came to a screeching halt to avoid colliding with the wooden fence. Bianca went soaring right over it!

Luckily, Turo had quick reflexes. He leaped forward and caught her. "You okay, little buddy?"

"That. Was," Bianca replied, wide-eyed. "Awesome!"

The PALs sighed in relief. Al Granger, who had been watching the scene from inside Pru's house, rushed outside to check on Bianca. He brought his first-aid kit and helped Bianca bandage up the one small scrape she had gotten when her knee brushed the wooden fence.

"Maybe it would be best if you girls gave the training a rest," Mr. Granger suggested. He didn't look too happy. "I hate to say it, but maybe Mr. Rollins was right. You should just leave Sandy alone until he comes to pick her up on Founders' Day. She might be too much for you girls to handle."

"Dad, no!" Pru protested. "We can do this. We've only been trying for a few days."

"Sandy just needs more time!" Abigail added.

Mr. Granger finally agreed under one condition—they had to take regular breaks. Sandy was probably just too overwhelmed and confused to figure things out. The PALs admitted that he had a point.

As soon as Turo, Mr. Granger, Snips,

and the twins all left, the girls suddenly felt exhausted. They brought Sandy back to the barn, undid her tack, and began to brush her down.

"So Sandy's not a packhorse and she's not a riding horse," Lucky conceded, feeling discouraged. She couldn't bear to give up on the little horse now. Lucky was positive that Sandy was meant for something special. She reached out and brushed her fingers through Sandy's soft mane. "What kind of horse are you, girl?"

A true Trail Trainer wouldn't give up that easily. One way or another, you could bet your bridle that Lucky would figure it out.

Chapter 7

Chica Linda, Boomerang, and Spirit seemed to be enjoying the trails even more than usual today. The horses had spent a lot of time in the muggy barn recently, so the girls promised to take them out for an extra-long ride. As they rode across the wild terrain, Spirit led the way. He took them on a brand-new route that followed the path of a pretty stream, lined with patches of purple and yellow flowers under shady trees. The girls made lots of stops to rest, eat snacks, and wade through the cool waters. Summer truly felt as if it were just around the corner.

Still, Lucky couldn't help thinking about Sandy back at home, even though she tried her hardest to push the training dilemma from her mind and enjoy the trail ride with her best friends. She knew that Sandy was safe with Buster the Clydesdale and Mr. Granger. She was probably doing her signature twirl and trying to beg Al for treats like a puppy at this very moment.

On the way back, Pru noticed that their route would take them right past the Calloway Barn on the outskirts of Miradero. The Calloway Barn was enormous and was no longer used to keep horses, so old

Mr. Calloway was kind enough to let the townspeople of Miradero build and store their Founders' Day Parade floats there in preparation for the big day. That way, everything would be a surprise. Of course, Maricela had gone to nose around at the barn last year. She had delighted in telling everyone that she knew exactly what the floats were before they did. Pru didn't care much about that, but it did sound like a really cool and interesting thing to see.

"Let's stop and take a look around," Pru insisted as the barn came into sight. "Please?" Lucky and Abigail didn't protest, as long as they weren't going to get in trouble for looking. The girls crept to the big barn door and stood to the side to peer in.

The floats were magnificent. Some were covered in paper flowers, like the one in the shape of a giant basket with daisies tumbling out. Others had painted scenes of the founding of Miradero on the sides, surrounded by ribbons and fringed streamers. But Mr. Winthrop's float looked like a cloud with a big red orb in the middle. Not quite as cool as the one from when Pru was seven.

"Oh, I get it!" Abigail nodded. "It's scoops of vanilla with a cherry on top! He just hasn't added the stem yet." Suddenly, a guy carrying a big curved red stick walked past and attached it to the top of the ball. But it wasn't just any guy—it was Turo!

"Hi, girls," Turo said.

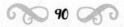

"What are you doing here?" Pru asked.

"I agreed to build parts for some of the floats, so I'm just making a few deliveries and helping out where I can," he replied. "Wanna take a look with me?" The PALs all nodded wildly.

As Turo showed them around, Lucky felt a weird mixture of emotions. She had a mounting sense of excitement for the parade, but also dread at the thought that Sandy might have to be given back. "Who's riding up front this year?" Abigail whispered to Turo as they admired the "basket of flowers" float. "Do you know?"

"I think it's a surprise. No one knows who's even *choosing* the riders." Turo shrugged and changed the subject. "Hey, how is Sandy doing? I see she's not out on the trail ride with you."

"She's just resting today," explained Lucky. She forced a smile. "Then we'll try again with a new training style tomorrow. It seems as if Sandy really doesn't like carrying too much on her back. But she's so strong!"

"Hmmm..." Turo looked around thoughtfully. "What if instead of carrying

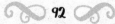

something, Sandy *pulled* something? If she's
as strong as you say she is, do you think she
would be good with a cart?" He pointed to
a row of old wagons that were once used for

hauling goods. They still had attachments
on the sides so that they could hitch to a
horse's saddle.

It was exactly the reason Mr. Granger
bought Buster—to be a draft horse and to
pull things like wagons—but the girls had

never considered that job for Sandy. Even though she was so strong, she was so tiny that the idea almost sounded silly! But what if it was just silly enough to work?

"I think it's worth a shot!" Lucky wasn't about to turn down another work style. She would do anything to get this horse trained. Plus, she knew Mr. Granger would be really impressed if Sandy was able to help around the stables. "Do you think you could help us build something small enough?"

"I'm on it!" Turo cheered. He put his hands on his hips triumphantly. "I love a challenge."

Apparently, Lucky, Abigail, and Pru did, too.

Chapter 8

When they arrived back at the barn, the
PALs had a surprise guest waiting for them.
"Caroline!" Lucky called out and waved.
"What are you doing here?"

"Hey there, everyone!" Caroline lit up
when she caught sight of Spirit, Chica
Linda, and Boomerang trotting toward her.
"I thought I'd get some fresh air in between
piano lessons. It's such a gorgeous day."

"You can hang out with us for a while
if you'd like." Pru smiled and dismounted

from Chica Linda. "Wait out here for a minute while we brush these guys down. Then you can meet Sandy!"

Caroline beamed. "I can't wait!"

After getting their horses settled in the barn, Lucky and Pru headed back out to Caroline.

"We should probably warn you that Sandy can be a bit wild," Lucky advised.

"Like Spirit?" Caroline asked, confused. But as soon as Abigail released Sandy from her stall, it all made sense. The miniature horse burst out of the barn, full of energy. She kicked out her legs and galloped in circles. She twirled again and again before shaking her mane and giving a high-pitched whinny. The PALs all jumped into

the pen to try and wrangle the little horse.

"She's so funny!" Caroline clapped her hands together in delight as she watched the horse evade the capture attempts by Abigail, Pru, and Lucky.

"Maybe you *are* a performing horse, Sandy!" Abigail called out, trying to corner Sandy near some barrels. "Look at you, entertaining the audience. Now, be a good horsey and—*oof!*"—Abigail tripped over her shoe and stumbled against a barrel as Sandy went careening toward the other side of the ramada—"hold still." Abigail sighed, watching her run off again.

This time, however, was different. Sandy burst through the fence's wooden gate—and headed right for Caroline! Lucky sprang into action, chasing after her. "Sandy, *whoaaa!*" she shouted at the top of her lungs. "Whoa!" The voice command hadn't worked yet, so she wasn't confident it would this time, either.

But something miraculous happened. Sandy stopped! Her hooves skidded to a halt just before she reached Caroline. "Easy, girl," Caroline said softly. Sandy took two steps forward. "That's it. Easy..." The little horse inched even closer until finally she was near enough to bend her muzzle down to Caroline. Caroline smiled as she petted Sandy's face and scratched behind her ear. Sandy snorted happily.

Sandy was *listening*! Lucky's jaw dropped. "Are you guys seeing this?!" she whispered to Abigail and Pru, careful not to disturb the moment. When Lucky glanced over at them, expressions of shock registered on their faces, too. Sandy regarded Caroline with a gentle sweetness that she hadn't displayed all week. She was totally calm and collected.

"Let's try something...." Pru rushed over and picked up Sandy's rope lead, which was dragging on the ground. Pru then instructed Caroline to wheel forward alongside her and the horse. Sure enough, Sandy walked slowly beside them. When Caroline stopped, she stopped. Then the horse just stared at Pru for the next command.

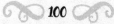

"Whoa," breathed Abigail. "What is happening?"

They'd tried so many different tactics to train Sandy so far, but none of them had worked. Now she was responding to this new friend as if they'd known each other for years. This was exactly the demeanor Lucky and her friends had been trying to draw out of the wild little horse. The wheels in Lucky's head were spinning. This was their chance. They wouldn't have to return Sandy to Mr. Rollins. The PALs could succeed in becoming Trail Trainers!

"Caroline, I hope you're not busy after your next piano lesson," Lucky said, practically bubbling over with joy. "'Cause we have a lot of training to do with Sandy and we could use your help. I can't believe how much she loves you!"

"Sign me up!" Caroline replied with the biggest smile. Maybe Miradero wouldn't be so boring this summer after all.

Chapter 9

Over the next few days, the PALs got up early each morning to put in time with Sandy alone while Caroline taught piano lessons. Then in the afternoon, she would come to the ramada to feed Sandy treats and give her encouragement while the PALs taught her new skills. They were making incredible progress so far. It was as if a switch had been flipped once Sandy met the young teacher, and now there was no turning back. Sandy was a star student—

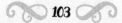

and with Caroline's help, the girls were becoming star trainers!

Today, Abigail was helping Lucky teach Sandy the voice commands of "walk," "canter," and "trot" to medium success. Sandy had definitely perfected "walk" and "whoa," but more complicated commands still eluded her. Also, their horse treat supply was running dangerously low, much to Boomerang's and Chica Linda's dismay.

By the time Caroline finally arrived, Sandy was refusing to practice any more runs. When she saw Caroline, she went trotting up to the side of the pen to meet her. Sandy gave Caroline her usual greeting of nuzzling Caroline's neck and sniffing her braids. "Hello to you, too." Caroline laughed. "Sandy, I'm so proud of you. You've come so far in your training."

"Not far enough," Lucky admitted with a sigh. "She can still be so unpredictable."

"I think I have a solution to that," Caroline said. She reached inside her satchel and pulled out a stack of papers. She passed one to Abigail, Pru, and Lucky. At the top, in pretty cursive, it read *SANDY LESSON PLAN.*

"What's this?" Lucky read aloud. "'Visualization, Learning by Example, Small Steps Equal Great Strides...?'"

"Well, I can't help you much in the way of actual horse training," Caroline explained. "But I *am* a teacher. And I've had lots of students." She pointed to Lucky's

paper. "These are some of the techniques
that work whenever we are trying to
prepare for a big piano concert. Maybe
Sandy would be more consistent if we
treated her more like a student!"

Pru and Abigail loved the idea. Lucky,
however, felt a bit hesitant about it all.
If they suddenly changed their methods
again just when they were starting to work,

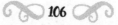

wouldn't it only confuse Sandy? Lucky really liked Caroline and Sandy seemed to like her, too, but she didn't know very much about horses. A piano lesson with a child was not the same thing as training an animal. But the thought of that shiny Frontier Fillies Trail Trainer emblem popped up in her mind and prompted Lucky to say, "Sure, let's give it a try."

They started with the Visualization section. According to Caroline, if you pictured yourself being successful at the thing you were trying to accomplish in your head, you would actually be able to do it in real life. Pru was familiar with this method. Apparently, she used it herself for dressage competitions all the time. But getting Sandy to picture herself cantering across the pen was a little trickier.

"Maybe if we all picture Sandy doing the canter at the same time, she will get the message...*uhh*...telepathically?" Abigail suggested, tilting her head to the side.

"Or we could just start with an easier one. How about 'Learning by Example'? Often, one of the best ways to learn is to watch someone else play the song first—oops! I mean, watch another horse do it first." Caroline pointed to where Chica Linda, Boomerang, and Buster were all hitched up, watching the lesson. "Pru, can Chica Linda do all the commands?"

"Of course she can!" Pru nodded. She reached over to pet Chica Linda's soft

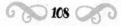

mane, beaming with pride. "My girl is amazing. Plus, I've had her since I was eight. We've had time on our side."

Pru unhitched Chica Linda and led her inside the pen with Sandy. The two horses greeted each other, ears twitching and rocking their heads back. Lucky jumped inside, eager to help. "Let's start with 'walk' and then we'll do 'back.'"

"Walk, Chica Linda!" Pru directed as she herself walked backward in front of the mare. Chica Linda obliged, looking rather bored. Pru gave her a treat. Then it was Lucky and Sandy's turn. Having just seen Chica Linda do the trick and receive a treat for doing so, Sandy got it on the first try.

"Bingo!" shouted Abigail, jumping up

and down. "Brilliant idea, Caroline!"

After a few more tests, they all agreed that the strategy was working. Lucky was feeling pretty good. But after watching how Sandy responded to Caroline specifically praising her, Pru suggested they try something new. "I think I've finally figured out what kind of horse Sandy is. Our training methods haven't really been clicking with Sandy. They really only work when Caroline is around. So maybe she's not a packhorse, a riding horse, a performing horse, or even a draft horse...." Pru led Sandy over to Caroline. She put her hands out toward them as if they were the main act of a show. "She's a companion horse!"

"What's that?" Abigail asked, skipping

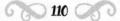

over to them. "I've never heard of a companion horse before. Do they do chores or something?"

"Not exactly." Pru shook her head. "Sandy has such a natural connection with Caroline. She just wants to be with her all the time. Kinda like our horses with us."

Lucky couldn't argue with that one. She often felt as if she and Spirit had a bond that nobody else could truly understand.

"So I figure—why don't we train Sandy to be Caroline's companion? They were clearly meant for each other! She could even help Caroline with everyday tasks instead of all this other stuff." Pru walked over to the gate on the fence and opened it. "We could start off by teaching her to open gates and doors." She turned to Caroline. "What do you think?"

"I think it would be amazing!" Caroline squealed. She reached forward to pet Sandy, who started to whinny from all the excitement. She wriggled to and fro and tugged on the ropes that held her as Abigail and Pru began to brainstorm other things to teach Sandy that would relate to her new role as a companion horse.

Lucky felt a bit frustrated. Of course, it was a great idea. But they were running out of time and they had just finally started to make progress on some of the traditional training. What if the reason Sandy hadn't gotten it yet was because they kept switching things on her? And now with only three days left until Mr. Rollins's arrival Pru had come up with yet another new plan.

"No!" Lucky found herself saying, interrupting the celebration. "We can't do that. We don't have time!" Everyone stopped talking, stunned.

"Of course we do, Lucky," Abigail replied gently. "It'll be okay."

Lucky frowned. "But if we don't prove to Mr. Rollins that Sandy is fully trained, we won't be able to keep her. Not us, not Caroline—nobody!"

"Is this about Trail Trainers?" Pru asked.

"No!" Lucky folded her arms across her chest. "Not at all!" Something tugged at Lucky's heart. Maybe it was about becoming a Trail Trainer just a little bit, but she didn't want to admit it. She cared about Caroline, but Lucky was tired of everyone not being on the same page. She knew it would only end in disaster.

And it did. Just not in the way Lucky was expecting. As the girls got distracted with their conversation, they had failed to notice

that Sandy had managed to wriggle free from the rope tied to her harness. Before anyone could grab her, Sandy leaped out of reach and galloped toward the wilderness without looking back.

The little horse was gone and Lucky had only herself to blame.

Chapter 10

Lucky held tightly to Spirit's mane as she scanned the horizon, heart beating fast. "Sandy!" she shouted. "Where'd you go, girl?" But all that she saw was the same familiar landscape of trees, winding streams, and dusty plains. Not a miniature horse in sight. How could one tiny horse get so far, so quickly? Lucky silently beat herself up for getting so caught up in her goal of becoming a Trail Trainer and pushing Sandy so hard. Everyone learned at their own pace—horses included.

And now Sandy had run away.

What would they tell Mr. Rollins once he came to see Sandy's progress? Lucky cringed at the thought of delivering the news that not only had the three of them failed to train Sandy like they'd claimed they could, but that they were such inexperienced trainers that they'd actually gone and lost the horse!

Lucky saw Pru and Chica Linda in the distance and steered Spirit in their direction. After Sandy had run off, they'd grabbed some oats and quickly saddled up Boomerang and Chica Linda, but Lucky had been able to hop on Spirit faster. So she'd gone ahead. Caroline had agreed to

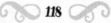

stay at the ramada in case Sandy made her way back there.

"Have you seen anything?" Lucky shouted to Pru, any disagreement between them having melted away into panic. "I did a sweep of the east side, but it's all quiet."

Pru shook her head. "Let's catch up with Abigail." They took off at a gallop westward, in the direction of the canyons.

When they reached her, Abigail confirmed what they already feared. There was no sign of Sandy.

"What are we going to do?" Lucky called out. "We need a plan."

"We should do one more sweep of the immediate area," Pru directed. "Make sure to look behind bushes and anyplace Sandy could hide."

After searching under the brush and inside caves, the girls began to realize that the chances of finding their runaway were not great. As they trotted back to Miradero, they felt beyond dreadful. Everything seemed pretty rotten.

At least there was one thing Lucky could do to make things right. They were

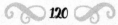

almost to the stables when she blurted out her apology. "I'm sorry for the way I acted earlier! I don't know what came over me. I guess I just wanted to succeed so badly that I lost sight of what we were trying to do in the first place: help Sandy find her true calling."

"I'm sorry, too," Pru replied. "You were right. We were confusing her with changing everything so often."

"And I'm sorry about running out of oat biscuits," Abigail joked to lighten the mood. "We all make mistakes."

The girls agreed to stay on the same page from now on—including doing something they all really didn't want to do. They had to tell Mr. Granger that Sandy was missing. They were trying their best to muster up the courage as they approached the barn. But as they got closer, they realized they didn't have to. Caroline met them by the trail, frantically waving.

"Lucky! Abigail! Pru!" she yelled. "Hurry! Sandy's been spotted near the Calloway Barn!"

"We're on it!" Lucky shouted, steering Spirit back in the other direction.

Chapter 11

A wide circle of people had formed around
Sandy outside the Calloway Barn, hoping
to help wrangle the horse and also protect
the floats from destruction. She kicked and
whinnied, stomped and snorted. She was
scared.

"Don't spook her!" Turo said insistently,
breaking through the crowd. "I know this
horse. Sandy is stronger than she looks!
Does anyone have any food?"

"We do!" shouted the PALs, arriving just

in the nick of time. "And she'll listen to us."

Abigail, Lucky, and Pru dismounted from their horses and carefully entered the circle. "It's okay, Sandy..." Lucky cooed. Sandy started twirling around frantically and shook her mane unhappily. The PALs inched closer, gently trying to calm Sandy down.

"C'mon, girl," Abigail said, holding out a treat. "Come here, please?" Sandy just backed up and gave a high-pitched whinny in response.

"Lucky!" The crowd parted around Caroline as she rolled her wheelchair into the circle. The moment Sandy noticed Caroline, she began to walk around the perimeter of the circle. Then she backed

up and began again, this time going into a trot.

"What's she doing?" Abigail frowned. "She's just going in circles...."

"Lucky!" Pru exclaimed with a smile. "She's doing the training practices! Sandy remembers what we taught her!"

Though it hardly seemed real, Pru was right. All those lessons and failed attempts at teaching the little horse had soaked in after all, even though she didn't want to listen to the PALs. Something just clicked when Caroline was there! Lucky felt as if her heart was bursting with pride for Sandy.

But she was still technically on the loose.

Like a beautifully choreographed dance, the PALs called out commands to the little

horse with Caroline cheering for her on the sidelines. Sandy performed each one with style. As the girls directed her, Sandy cantered, galloped, walked, and stopped. After each move, the crowd became more and more delighted. They cheered and clapped, and the miniature horse wasn't even scared anymore. Sandy's capture

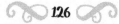

had turned into an accidental spectacle—a training display showcase.

As the PALs finished with their commands, Caroline rolled toward them. Immediately, Sandy was alert. She neighed happily and trotted over, meeting Caroline right in the middle. Then the horse leaned forward and licked her cheek. It was then that Lucky understood. This had all been for a reason, and it wasn't for them to become Trail Trainers.

"What exactly is going on here?" yelled a voice. Mr. Rollins broke through the crowd, looking stressed. "I heard my Sandy escaped! Where is she? I'm taking her back!"

"Mr. Rollins!" Pru rushed forward,

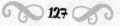

scrambling to explain. "She did escape, but—uh, we have it totally handled now." She gestured to Sandy and Caroline. "As you can see."

"It's true! Sandy has learned so much with us," Lucky added. "This is her new friend Caroline. We think Sandy'd be the perfect companion horse for her." Lucky turned to Caroline. "Pru was right, Caroline. You two were definitely meant for each other. I never should have doubted that, and I'm sorry."

Caroline smiled warmly. "It's okay, Lucky. You just wanted what was best for Sandy."

"And I think this is best," Lucky replied. "Mr. Rollins, what do you think?"

Sandy walked alongside Caroline as Caroline rolled her wheelchair forward. When she rolled back, so did Sandy. Everyone cooed at how sweet it was.

"Well, I'll be…" Mr. Rollins smiled and removed his cowboy hat. "I've never seen my little scoundrel Sandy so calm and well-behaved."

"And *I've* never seen such a compelling Trail Trainers demonstration!" announced a new voice.

Immediately, the girls whipped around. They were greeted by the sight of none other than *the* Ms. Hungerford, the very lady they needed to impress. How had she known to come to Miradero at all?

"You look surprised to see me," said

Ms. Hungerford with a smirk. "But you should ask your friend Abigail. She wrote to me a couple of weeks ago and said today was the day you would be doing your demonstration."

Pru and Lucky turned to Abigail, who was blushing deep crimson. "Oh yeah, I kinda forgot I did that."

"Well, no mind anyhow. I've seen more than enough to know that you three are true Trail Trainers. I'll see you at the next Jamboree." And with that, Ms. Hungerford turned on her heel and left.

"I can't believe the progress you've made with Sandy. She'll be the perfect companion horse. You girls sure proved yourselves to be skilled trainers," Mr. Rollins said, taking

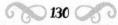

a step forward and petting Sandy. "How about your riding skills? They just as good?" He pointed to the floats. "That business I'm attending to? One of my old friends asked me to choose the riders for the front of the parade this year. Are the four of ya interested?" He gave Caroline a wink.

"Are we interested?!" Pru screeched, jumping up and down. "In leading the Founders' Day Parade?! Are you kidding me?" Lucky, Abigail, and Caroline joined in the squealing.

"I'll take that as a yes." Mr. Rollins laughed. "But there's just one thing left to settle first."

"What?" Lucky asked, bubbling over with happiness.

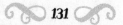

Mr. Rollins laughed as he said it: "Where is that apple pie I was promised?"

Chapter 12

The four girls stared at themselves in the dressing tent mirror and giggled. It was funny to see themselves in the traditional outfits of the first Miradero settlers, but they couldn't be prouder. Pru, especially, had dreamed of the day that she would be chosen to ride up front in the Founders' Day Parade for such a long time. She tugged on her bonnet and posed. "We look just like founders!"

"We sure do," Caroline agreed, looking

cheery in her mint-green frock. "But we'd better get a move on. They can't start without us, since we're going to be at the front and everything." She rolled outside to where Sandy was waiting. Sandy neighed happily when she saw Caroline. The horse was hitched up to the special wagon that Turo had built just for her. When he saw the demonstration with Caroline, he got right to work and changed its design so it could

safely hold Caroline's wheelchair.

Once everyone was saddled up and Caroline was secured in the wagon, the girls made their way to the staging area. The brilliant floats were lined up and ready to go. Abigail's saddlebag was even filled with mountains of confetti and sweets to throw out to the parade watchers. The excitement around town was palpable as the parade music began to play. Abigail, Pru, Lucky, and Caroline took their spots at the front.

"Ready, everyone?" Lucky looked to her friends, beaming with pride and honor. They still had a lot to learn, but she knew that they belonged there. They were skilled riders *and* trainers, but most important,

they embodied the spirit of the Miradero founders. They had forged ahead, trying new things and being brave enough to continue in the face of a challenge. And best of all, they'd done it together.

"Okay, Sandy...now canter!" Caroline called out, pulling her reins. But Sandy didn't budge. Pru, Abigail, and Lucky held their breaths. Then suddenly—the little horse took off! The people cheered as Sandy and Caroline turned onto the main road, leading the parade and showing the town of Miradero that with a little persistence, anything was possible.

G. M. (Gillian) Berrow is also the author of many My Little Pony chapter books and middle-grade novels, including the beloved in-world book series, the Daring Do Adventures. She loves writing about ponies and horses, playing with her mini poodle, and making puns.

Born in La Plata, Argentina, **Maine Diaz** grew up drawing and painting. Cartoons captured her imagination early on, and she realized immediately that she wanted to be an animator when she grew up. At the age of sixteen, Maine took a workshop and started animating. Soon after, she started illustrating for children's storybooks and educational books.

Currently, Maine lives in a tiny green house, where she spends time with her two cats, Chula and Lola. When not illustrating, she enjoys swimming, writing, and taking photos.